# The Little Drummer Boy ™

Retold by Irene Trimble
Illustrated by Linda Karl

D1384747

 **A GOLDEN BOOK • NEW YORK**

Copyright © 2003 by Random House, Inc. All rights reserved under International and Pan-American Copyright Conventions. Published in the United States by Golden Books, an imprint of Random House Children's Books, a division of Random House, Inc., New York, and simultaneously in Canada by Random House of Canada Limited, Toronto. Golden Books, A Golden Book, and the G colophon are registered trademarks of Random House, Inc. Based upon "The Little Drummer Boy" animated program © 1968, renewed 1996 by Classic Media, Inc. Character names, images, and other indicia are trademarks of Classic Media, Inc.   Library of Congress Control Number: 2002115313

www.goldenbooks.com

ISBN: 0-375-82625-4

10 9 8 7 6 5 4 3 2 1

Once there was a little orphan boy named Aaron. He lived in the desert with his animal friends, Joshua the camel, Samson the mule, and Baba the lamb.

Aaron loved to play his drum. It had been given to him by his parents. And because it was a gift of love, it had a magical quality. His animal friends danced whenever they heard it!

One day, Ben Haramad, the king of the desert showmen,
and his assistant Ali saw Aaron and his dancing animals.
"With this marvel in my show, I will be rich!" Ben said as
he forced Aaron and his animals to travel to the city with him.

A crowd quickly gathered in the city. Ben told Aaron to smile
and play his drum. But Aaron would not smile, so Ben painted
one on Aaron's face.

Aaron played his drum and performed for the crowd.
They cheered and yelled for more!

"Play it again!" Ben told the boy. But Aaron refused, and
the crowd became angry. They chased Ben and all his
performers out of the city and into the desert.

In the desert, Ben spotted a camp with three kings.

"What luck! One performance and I'll set you free!" Ben promised Aaron. He hoped the kings would pay him to hear the drummer boy play.

But the kings didn't have time to listen. They were packing up
camp to follow a star that would bring them to the newborn king.

The kings loaded their camels with precious gifts of gold, frankincense, and myrrh. But one of their camels couldn't hold the heavy load.
"Ben has a camel," said one of the kings. "Perhaps he would sell it."

Ben quickly sold Joshua the camel to the kings.

Aaron had to find Joshua. But he didn't know which way to go. Then he remembered that the three kings were following a star. "If we follow it, we're sure to catch up with them!" Aaron told Baba and *Samson*.

Aaron, Baba, and Samson followed the shining star to the tiny town of Bethlehem. Many shepherds had followed the star, too. They were all gathered in front of a baby in a manger, and they were all bearing gifts.

Aaron spotted the three kings—and his camel Joshua!

Aaron's heart was so full of joy that he ran into the road
calling, "Joshua!"

But suddenly, a chariot came around the corner and struck
little Baba down.

Aaron picked Baba up in his arms. "Who will help me?" he asked.
Then he looked toward the manger. "The kings are wise," Aaron
said. "They will be able to save Baba!"

Aaron brought his lamb over to one of the kings. The king looked at Baba and shook his head because there was nothing he could do.

But he told Aaron there was a king among kings who could save
her. Then he pointed to the baby in the cradle. "Go to him," he said.
"Look upon the newborn king."

Aaron laid Baba down and walked to the manger.
He wondered what gift he could give to the baby king.

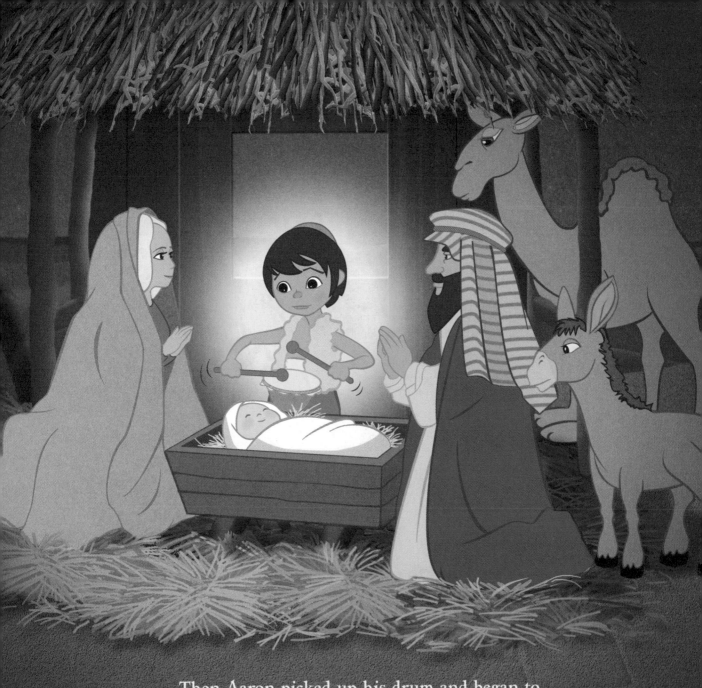

Then Aaron picked up his drum and began to
play with all his heart.

"Your gift, little drummer boy, given out of the simple desperation of a pure love, is the one favored above all," the king said. Then he pointed to the little lamb.

Baba jumped into Aaron's arms.
She was well and happy!

Joshua, Samson, and Baba danced while Aaron
played his drum.
At last, the friends were all together again!